Introduction

This story *The Adventures of Russell the Service Dog* is inspired by a real dog name Russell. He was born in Juneau Alaska on September 14th, 2014 and began his life living in a group home for individuals with developmental disabilities. While working with K.A.Marabel he was able to bring joy to her clients. During his life, Russell brought joy to many people from Alaska to Kentucky. Russell never met a person or animal he did not like. Some of his favorite hobbies were swimming, snuggling, fetch and hiking. Russell passed away unexpectedly on June 28th 2021. He is missed.

The Adventures of Russell the Service Dog

2nd Edition

K.A.Marabel

Copyright

Dedication

To Russell,

The best companion anyone could have asked for.

I miss our adventures together.

Contents

Epigraph ... IX

1. Super Russ ... 1

2. First Day ... 10

3. Lunchroom Woes ... 22

4. Field Day ... 37

5. Pop Quiz ... 47

6. Cheater, Cheater ... 65

7. Hemmed Capes ... 87

8. Helping Paw ... 96

9. Missing Star ... 106

10. Skipping School ... 117

11. Max Maxwell Episode 17: Part 2 ... 134

12. 15 Facts About Service Dogs 144

Acknowledgements 147

Also By 148

About the Author 149

"You don't have to be a super hero to know how to help"

-Mr. Henry

Chapter One
Super Russ

POW!

BANG!

CRASH!

Super Mutt spun around with a swift kick.

POW!

The robbers soared through the air and crashed through the window of the police station across from the bank. Super Mutt smacked his paws together, sending a small cloud of white dust into the air before placing his paws on his hips as his red cape blew in the breeze.

"No dog robs a bank in my city."

Super Mutt turned back towards the bank as his ears lifted. He heard a ticking sound, then his eyes grew wide.

"A bomb." He barked as he placed his paws on his temples, activating his super hearing as he tilted his head. His super hearing high-lighted a pulsing coming from the back of the bank, near the vicinity of the banker's office. Super Mutt activated his super vision to count the hostages through the walls of the bank where they laid tied up on the marble floor.

"Seven hostages," Super Mutt barked as he scanned again for the bomb. Without wasting time, Super Mutt jumped through the half-shattered bank window and ran down the hall towards the banker's office, sending a gust of wind behind him, knocking the pictures off the wall as he ran by.

Super Mutt grabbed the door with the glass that read "Chief Banker" and gave the knob a jerk, accidentally ripping it from its hinges.

"Whoops, guess I do not know my strength."

Super Mutt set the door against the wall and placed his hands on his temples to activate his super hearing. His eyes grew wide as he heard the ticks pulsing from the bottom draw of the banker's filing cabinet. Super Mutt's jaw dropped when he opened the draw and saw...

"Uh, I hate commercials."

Russell placed his paws on the TV screen, barking at the guy in the Liver Nips commercial.

"I thought you were supposed to be in bed twenty minutes ago."

"But Ma, Super Mutt still has a bomb to find. Just five more minutes, Ma." Russell stared at his mom, tail wagging. She placed her knitting down on the couch beside her.

"Right after, you need to head to bed, you have a big day tomorrow."

Russell's high-pitched yips filled the living room as he ran a circle around the coffee table before returning to the television to assume his normal viewing position. His tail wagged as a Great Dane in a suit came on the television, cleared his throat, and spoke. Russell tilted his head to the side.

"Good evening," the anchorman said, "I am Nip Ankleman and we interrupt your regularly scheduled broadcast to bring you breaking news…"

"No, Super Mutt has a bomb to find, gr-rrr." Russell growled and barked at the news broadcaster until the TV screen went black. Russell tilted his head to the side, staring at the black screen until he looked towards his mom, holding the remote and tapping her paw on the carpet.

"Looks like Super Mutt will have to find the bomb another day," she gently barked.

Russell whined as he placed his front paws back on the carpet and trudged towards the stairs, grumbling, "If I was Super Mutt, I would have already found the bomb."

"I'm sure you would. Don't forget to brush your teeth."

Russell yawned. He crawled under his Super Mutt blanket and held his Super Mutt plush in the air, making him fly as he let out another yawn. "What if I was a superhero?" Russell mumbled to his plush. He then pretended his plush spoke back.

"Nice to meet you, Super Russ," Russell grumbled in a deep voice, as if Super Mutt was responding, wiggling his head back and forth. Russell let out a yawn and rolled towards the window. Unable to fight sleep any longer, Russell imagined he was a hero called Super Russ.

POW!

BANG!

SMASH!

Super Russ punched the robbers, sending them flying and crashing into the police station window. Super Russ adjusted his red cape and looked at the broken glass on the sidewalk. It glistened in the sun like confetti. "No pup robs banks in my town."

Super Russ wiped the sweat off his brow and turned towards the bank. His ears perked up as he heard a ticking coming from within the bank. He looked through the window at all the hostages laying on the wood floor.

"A bomb."

Super Russ placed his paws on his temple, activating his super vision, counting the hostages. "One...three...seven—Seven hostages."

Super Russ adjusted his cape before diving through the broken window of the bank and running past the three hostages as he followed the sound of ticking. The ticking speed increased as Super Russ threw open the office door, where a large bomb sat on the desk. He ran up to the bomb and looked at the timer attached to the dynamite. The ticking sped up even faster.

Tick.

Tick Tick.

Tick Tick Tick.

Tick Tick Tick Tick Tick Tick.

Super Russ' heart raced as he snatched the bomb off the banker's desk. His paws shaking, he ran past the bound hostages while the timer ticked faster and faster. He made it to the broken window with a few seconds to spare.

05.

04.

03.

Super Russ leaped out of the broken window, but his cape snagged on the glass, sending him flying back into the bank as all the hostages screamed.

AHHH!

Tick.

Tick.

BOOM!

Chapter Two

First Day

BUZZZ!

Russell sat straight up in bed, panting as he watched his bedroom door slowly creaking open, a shadow appeared on his wall.

"Good morning."

Russell let out a sigh as his mom shut off his alarm, relieved it was only her. Russell threw off his covers and stood on his bed. His tail wagged and he danced back and forth on the covers, waiting for his mom to help him down.

"Today is the big day," she said, helping him down from his bed. A smile spread across his face and his eyes grew wide when he remembered what today was.

"Wait!" he cried. Russell wiggled out of his mom's arms and sprinted towards his closet, struggling to gain traction on the hardwood floor before crashing into his closet door. "I'm okay."

Russell rubbed his nose before squeezing through his slightly jarred closet. His tail wagged as he dove headfirst into his toy box, sending toys flying left and right.

"What are you looking for?" his mom asked, ducking from a flying tennis ball.

"Got it!"

Russell emerged from the closet with his red cape hanging out of his mouth and a smile across his face. He ran to his mirror and fastened the slightly oversized cape around his neck. He placed his paws on his hips and raised his chin while looking at his reflection.

"Like Super Mutt." He nodded proudly at his reflection.

"Are you forgetting something?" his mom gently barked, pointing to his dresser. Russell's eyes lit up as he ran to his dresser and pulled open the bottom draw. His tail wagged as his back legs lifted off the ground as he leaned inside, pulling out his new red school vest. His mom smiled as she helped him adjust it. "Looks like you grew into it."

Russell ran to the mirror and held his chin up, admiring himself. He ran his paw across the embroidered words on his vest, reading them aloud.

"Service Dog in training."

A few minutes later, Russell's mom shouted from the kitchen, "Breakfast is ready." Russell tossed his Super Mutt toothbrush back into his cup and ran down the stairs, tripping halfway on his cape, sending him tumbling to the bottom and landing on his head.

"I'm okay," Russell grunted as he scooted himself up to the table. His mom placed an empty bowl in front of him.

"What flavor of kibble do you want?" His mom licked him on the top of the head as she waited for him to answer.

"You're messing up my fur," he grumbled as he patted his hair back down, wanting to look his best for his first day. "Liver Nips," Russell finally answered, grabbing the box from his mom. He noticed a picture of a missing pup on the back.

"Missing terrier pup...Trixie. Ma, there's a missing pup on my Liver Nips."

"I'm sure the search and rescue dogs are looking for her."

"And Super Mutt!"

Russell sniffed his bowl of kibble. His eyes grew large and he dove in headfirst, sending pieces flying all over the table and onto the rug. Russell's mom was watching him search for stray kibble when the bus squeaked to a stop in front of their doghouse.

HONK.

HONK HONK.

Russell lifted his head and looked at the door. As Russell tried to climb down off his chair, he slipped and landed on his belly. "Whoops."

Russell chuckled as he lifted himself up and attempted to run towards the door, sliding on the hardwood floor before skidding to a stop.

His mom gave his vest one final adjustment before she opened the door.

Russell flipped his cape back before taking off, running through the grass. Halfway across the lawn, Russell stepped on the corner of his cape, sending him tumbling. The students on the bus laughed, but Russell just stood up, straightened his cape, and climbed up the bus steps.

"Nice cape," a student at the back of the bus teased. Russell made his way to the only available seat, next to a golden-furred pup.

"May I sit with you?" Russell asked as he pointed to the empty seat next to her. She looked up from her book and nodded, sliding her pink backpack over to make room. Russell sat next to her and held out his paw.

"I'm Russell, but you can call me Russ." She reached out to shake his paw.

"Maddy, and it's nice to meet you," she told him as she pushed her glasses back up. Russell felt a tap on his shoulder and turned to the seat behind him.

"Why are you wearing that cape? Who do you think you are, Super Mutt or something?" The black-furred pup chuckled as he and his friends' laughter filled the bus. Russell felt a tug on his vest, and he turned and sat back down.

"Ignore them. I like your cape," Maddy mumbled with her face in her book. "Did you know service dogs improve the lives of thousands across the country?" she asked, pointing at a page in her textbook. Russell just shook his head as he pulled out his notebook and started doodling Super Mutt.

Russell squeezed through the crowded hall, trying to find his way to his new classroom.

His tail wagged when he noticed Maddy from the school bus sitting at the desk in the front of the classroom.

"Hey, is this your class, too?" Russell said as he wagged his tail.

"Yep, I guess it is."

"At least I know I have a friend," Russell told her as he sat at the desk next to her. After the bell rang, the teacher shut the door and walked to the whiteboard, where he wrote his name: Mr. Henry.

"Welcome, future service dogs," Mr. Henry quietly barked as all the pups began yipping and wagging their tails. "Settle down," he told them. "I will teach you the basics of being a service dog this semester, and we will start on our first assignment. You are to help a fellow student in need, and you each will earn a gold star." Mr. Henry pointed to the star chart on the wall.

"You are to earn a gold star each week if you want to pass this class," he added.

Russell's tail wagged as he pictured himself saving other students like Super Mutt would. Russell looked out the window as Mr. Henry's voice faded, daydreaming he was Super Russ again.

Super Russ stood overlooking Mount Ruff-more, observing the faces of dogs of the past. He watched as the sculptors on scaffolding chiseled away at his likeness. Super Russ stood with his hands on his hips, grinning from ear to ear.

"I better get to city hall," Super Russ said as he looked at his watch.

When he arrived, landing on city hall's marble steps, the crowd cheered. A corgi in a light blue suit stood at the podium and cleared his throat.

"Welcome everyone; as you know, I am Mayor Wagsworth."

The crowd cheered as Mayor Wagsworth waved for Super Russ to come to the podium. "Settle down, now," the mayor said, gesturing to the crowd. "As your duly elected mayor, I am proud to be here as you witness this glorious moment in *Dogwood* history."

Mayor Wagsworth began digging through his pockets, searching for something. "Just a moment," he said into the mic, before mumbling to himself, "Where is it?" His assistant leaned in and whispered in his ear as she handed him a box.

"Ah ha, here it is." He cleared his throat, picked up his cue card, and adjusted his mic as he read. "I invited everyone here to witness this rare event in our great town's history. I award Super Russ the gold star to the city."

The crowd barked and howled as mayor Wagsworth open the box, revealing the golden star within. The mayor took the star and pinned it to Super Russ' suit.

"Say a word for our townsfolk," Mayor Wagsworth said as he stepped towards the left. Super Russ approached the mic and cleared his throat as the crowd silently watched.

"Thank you, everyone," Super Russ said, and the crowd roared to life, chanting.

"Super Russ!"

"Super Russ!"

"Russ!"

Chapter Three
Lunchroom Woes

"RUSSELL," MADDY SAID AS she gave him a shake. Russell's eyes popped open, and he lifted his head off his desk.

"Huh?" he said, wiping drool off his mouth.

"It's lunchtime," Maddy said as she tugged on his vest to follow her. Russell got up and stretched and followed her to the front of the room. He stopped to look at his name on the star chart, picturing what it would be like to get a million gold stars and became a superhero like Super Mutt. He followed her out of the room and walked with her towards the cafeteria. Russell looked around at all the students, hoping one might need help.

"Russell. Oh Russell!"

"Um, what?" Russell said as he turned from looking over his shoulder.

"The cafeteria is over here." Maddy said as she raised her eyebrows and chuckled. Maddy held the door until Russell caught up. Russell stuck his nose in the air and sniffed. Liver Nips, he thought as his stomach growled as he entered the fragrant cafeteria. He followed Maddy into the lunch line. Russell panted as his mouth salivated while he watched each student before them get their bowls of kibble. He tried to make up his mind before he made it to the lunch lady. Maddy stood after she got her kibble and waited on Russell.

"What kind dear?" the grey-furred lunch lady asked, her paws shaking as she held the empty bowl.

"Both!" Russell yipped as his tail wagged. He stood with his mouth open as he watched her scoop a large ladle full of wet food and plop it into his bowl, and then topping it with a large scoop of dry food.

"Here you go, young man." The lunch lady said as her shaking paws handed Russell the over filled bowl.

Russell followed Maddy through the lunch line and sat down across the table from her. Russell stared at his bowl of kibble unable to wait as his stomach growled and his mouth drooled. He shoved his face into his bowl as Maddy opened her book to the page she crimped earlier. Maddy cleared her throat as she watched Russell chomping at the kibble.

"Did you know that each service dog has their own unique duties and responsibilities?" Maddy asked as she looked at Russell, who was making a mess of his kibble.

"Mmm hmm," Russell answered with a mouthful of kibble. Maddy watched as Russell sent dry kibble rolling all over the table and onto the floor as well as blobs of wet kibble on the table. Noticing that Maddy has barely touched her kibble, Russell asked with a full mouth, "You, okay?"

"I think I lost my appetite," Maddy sighed as she wiped kibble off her side of the table. Russell's eyes grew large as he looked at Maddy's bowl as he realized how he could help a student in need. He swallowed his last bite and jumped up onto their table. Maddy watched as Russell dove face first into her bowl, sending kibble flying.

"Ew," she yelped as she wiped kibble off her book. "Russ!" she barked, hoping to get him to stop, but Russell was too busy devouring her kibble to hear her.

Mr. Henry heard Maddy's yelps and walked over to their table to investigate. "What is going on?" he asked, pulling the half-empty bowl of kibble from Russell.

"He took her lunch," barked a student at the next table who pointed at Russell.

Russell looked at Mr. Henry with his cheeks full of kibble before shaking, sending kibble all over Mr. Henry and the cafeteria.

"Maddy, go get yourself a fresh bowl while I have a talk with Russell," Mr. Henry barked as he wiped kibble off his teacher's vest with his handkerchief.

Russell swallowed his mouthful and grinned, his cheeks turning red. "I'm helping

Maddy eat her lunch. Do I get a gold star now?" Russell panted as he watched Mr. Henry place his paws on his hips.

"Stealing is NOT helping," Mr. Henry barked as he tapped his paw on the cafeteria floor. Russell's smile quickly vanished as he tucked his tail between his legs and lowered his head. "I will let it go this time because today is your first day but next time, you will be in detention," Mr. Henry told Russell as he held up the half-empty bowl of kibble. Russell climbed down off the table and slumped back down in his seat feeling defeated.

Maddy returned with her fresh bowl. Russell said nothing while she picked at her kibble. Maddy tossed a piece at Russell for him to catch, but he missed, It bounced off his nose and landed on the floor, rolling to Mr. Henry's paw. Mr. Henry's glare made Russell slumped down in his seat and sit quietly until lunch was over. Russell tried to stay on Mr. Henry's good side the rest of the day.

On the way home, Russell's tail wagged as the bus came to a stop outside of his doghouse. He got off the bus and ran straight past his mom as she held their front door open. He rushed to the television and plopped down with his nose an inch from the screen. Russell's tail wagged as he looked at the black screen and back at his mom.

"Did I miss it, ma?" Russell barked as she followed him into the living room.

"You're just in time."

Russell watched his mom as she pointed and clicked the remote, turning on the television. His eyes grew wide and his tail wagged as his mom turned it to his favorite channel. His favorite show's music filled the living room as he stared into the TV screen.

Super Mutt took off his mask and cape and hung them on the hook on the wall. He looked at his reflection as he put on his black-rimmed glasses and adjusted his bow tie.

Ring...Ring...

"Maxwell here... Great, I will be right down." Max Maxwell hung up his phone and headed towards the door. He took the elevator down to the main floor and winked at the receptionist before walking through the revolving doors to his awaiting limousine. The doorman nodded as he walked past. The driver tipped his hat as he held the limousine door open. "Good evening, Mr. Maxwell."

"Evening Pugsley."

Max Maxwell slid into the limousine and adjusted his dress coat as leaned toward his date as the driver shut his door.

"Love the dress, Fifi. You put other Poodles to shame."

"Oh Maxwell, you are such the gentlemutt," she giggled as she briefly placed her hand on his paw.

"Ready for tonight?" he said as he took two crystal glasses from the minibar and poured them both a glass of cold spring water.

"I am always up for a good fundraiser, especially for an orphanage." Fifi said as she reapplied her bright red lipstick. The limousine came to a stop in front of a large columned building with the words *Chase City Town Hall*.

Fifi looked out the window at the cars lined down the block. "Look at all the paparazzi. They are just dying to snap a photo of the famous Max Maxwell of Maxwell Industries." She giggled as Max Maxwell shook his head and placed their glasses back on the minibar.

The driver pulled in front of the main entrance of the building and got out. He walked towards the back and opened the car door. Maxwell stepped out of the limousine, Fifi with him, holding his arm as the flash of the paparazzi's cameras made her red dress sparkle.

A news reporter approached Max Maxwell and held out a microphone. "Mr. Maxwell, can you tell our viewers if Fifi Frisbee will be the lucky dog to take you off the market?"

"As lovely as the beautiful Ms. Frisbee is, I am not ready to settle down just yet." Max Maxwell smiled at the camera before making his way up the red carpet through the large double doors with Fifi on his arm.

Fifi and Max Maxell danced in the ballroom as guests and paparazzi watched as they spun around the dance floor. The paparazzi cameras flashed as the couple could not take their eyes off each other.

"The evening has been highly successful. It will fund the orphanage for at least another year," Fifi said as Max gave her a twirl and dipped her just as the song ended.

"Excuse me, Fifi, there is one last guest I need to convince to open their wallet," Max Maxwell said as he handed her off to another gentledog. Maxwell approached a tall, well-groomed Poodle in a top hat.

"Ah, good evening, Mr. Maxwell. Your date makes us Poodles look good, does she not?" He chuckled while adjusting his monocle, watching her dance.

"Well, Mr. Goodfella, Perhaps I could arrange a dance between you two."

"Surely offering me a dance with your date is not why you are over here, is it, Mr. Maxwell?" Mr. Goodfella grinned as he took a sip of his drink.

"You are right. I will get to the point, Mr. Goodfella. Every dog here has donated to the orphanage but you."

"Ah, Maxwell, you have always had a soft spot for mutts just as yourself," Mr. Goodfella smirked.

"Must be your pedigree, Mr. Goodfella, that makes you such a snob. Perhaps I should talk to one of these reporters about how you refuse to help the orphanage and see how quick your stock drops."

"Now, there is no need for unpleasantries," Mr. Goodfella said as he reached into his dress coat pocket. He opened his checkbook and scribbled inside with his gold pen. "How is fifty thousand?"

"Thank you. How charitable of you," Max Maxwell said as he placed the check in the pocket of his dress coat as he glared at Mr. Goodfella.

"HELP...MAX!" screamed Fifi as a masked dog grabbed her from the dance floor as all the guests gasped.

"Where are you, Maxwell?" The masked figure taunted, shouting over the music. Max Maxwell ran to the dance floor as all the guests backed away, forming a circle around the perimeter as the music screeched to a stopped.

"What do you want?" Max Maxwell barked.

"Revenge," the masked figured barked as he tossed Fifi over his shoulder as she kicked and screamed. He pointed his grappling gun upward and pulled the trigger. Max Maxwell ran to stop him, but it was too late. The masked figure zipped up and out, sailing through the glass ceiling. The guests screamed as glass rained down on the dance floor and the screen faded to black with the words: To be continued...

"What?" Russell barked as the evening news started.

"Bedtime, honey," Russell's mom told him as she held the remote up, turning off the TV.

"The news always interrupts my show," Russell growled as he barked at the television.

"You are lucky I let you stay up this late to watch it."

"Yes, Ma," Russell said as he wrapped his paws around his mom's neck and she licks him on the nose. "Goodnight, Ma."

Chapter Four
Field Day

THE NEXT MORNING, RUSSELL sat in his bus seat and held the corner of his cape. He imagined he had hundreds of gold stars, one for every pup he had helped. Maddy read her textbook as Russell thought about the incident during lunch yesterday and whimpered to himself.

"You okay Russell?" Maddy asked as she looked up from her textbook.

"Yeah." Russell said as he looked out the window and watched the doghouses go by. It wasn't long before he was daydreaming again.

"HELP!" barked a boxer pup trapped in the window of an apartment building.

"HELP...FIRE," the pup barked again as he waved his paws in the air and smoke billowed out of his window towards the sky. Fire engine sirens blared in the distance as they struggled to get through rush hour traffic. The blaring siren echoed through the city and made its way to Super Russ' ears, awakening him from his afternoon nap. Super Russ ran to his window, unlatched it, and jumped out, soaring high into the night sky. In the distance, Super Russ spotted the smoke rising from the tall apartment building. He straightened his cape and flew towards the chaos.

Super Russ spotted the pup in the apartment window. The pup shouted, "Help! I'm over here." Super Russ looked around to see if there was any immediate danger as he prepared to fly into the window.

"Oh no," Super Russ mumbled to himself when he spotted the fire making its way to the propane tank that sat next to the brick wall on the outside of the building. Super Russ had no choice as he dove into the window and scooped up the pup. Bystanders cheered as Super Russ flew by.

BOOM.

The bystanders screamed as the propane tank exploded as they ducked to miss the flying debris. The entire building shook as a cloud of smoke rose into the air and debris fell on the streets. The explosion flung Super Russ across the street where he smashed into the window of the grocery store. The bystanders grew quiet as they watched for Super Russ to emerge from the wreckage.

With a groan, Super Russ opened his eyes. Something trapped him against a collapsed wall. He tightened his grip on the pup, who whimpered in his arms.

"Are you hurt?" Super Russ asked, looking at the pup, who shook his head as he clung to his fur. Super Russ leaned as he positioned his back paws against the collapsed wall. "I'll get you out of here."

He grunted as he attempted to lift the collapsed wall. He pushed with his back legs as hard as he could until the wall moved. The pup covered his eyes as the dust from the wall fell.

"GRRR!"

He growled as he sent the wall flying off them. He exhaled as he stood up and wiped dust and debris off the pup and himself. The bystanders cheered as Super Russ stepped through the window and landed down on the street below. Super Russ held the pup up and the crowd chanted.

"Super Russ!"

"Super Russ!"

"Russ!"

"Russ," Maddy chuckled as she looked up from her book and pushed her glasses back up. "Did you know service dogs can go through thousands of hours of schooling?"

she gently barked as the bus pulled into the school parking lot. They grabbed their things as the bus stop in front of the double doors.

"Today is a field day," Maddy reminded Russell as they stepped off the bus. "Maybe a student will need help," she added as she headed towards the field behind the school as Russell followed.

While walking to the playground to meet their teacher, Russell thought of rescuing a student caught in a tree or sinking in quicksand. Russell played on the swings with Maddy, but looked around in between pushing her, hoping to spot trouble.

"I can't do it," a student whined as he stood at the top of the tallest slide as he clung to the slide railing as his paws shook.

"Come on, don't be scaredy-cat," one pup teased as he watched from below.

"You're holding up the line," said another pup, holding onto the ladder, waiting to go up.

"Russell, are you going to push me?" Maddy said as her swinging slowly came to a stop.

"Someone is in trouble," Russell said before sprinting across the field. Maddy scooted off the swing and ran to catch up with him.

"Who's in trouble, Russell?" Maddy asked as she ran beside him.

"That pup up there. He's scared," Russell said, pointing towards the slide.

"Russell, I don't think he is…"

"Do not worry, Spot, I am here to help," Russell shouted as he adjusted his cape before climbing up the ladder forcing the other pups off.

"This should be good," a student teased while elbowing Maddy.

Russell made it to the top of the ladder. "I am here to help you," he told Spot.

Spot shook his head. "I'm okay, Russ."

Russell barked, "I'll help you down." He said as he gave Spot a shove, sending him flying down the long metal slide. Spot landed at the bottom, face first in the mud. All the students laughed at Spot as he sat up and wiped the mud off his terrified face. Maddy just shook her head at Russell, who was still on top of the slide. He had his paws on his hips and a proud look on his face as his cape danced in the breeze. Spot's yelps caught the attention of Mr. Henry who walked over to investigate.

"What happened? Are you okay?" Mr. Henry asked, pulling Spot out of the mud.

"Russell shoved me down the slide," Spot whined as he wiped mud off his vest and rubbed his nose, his eyes tearing up.

"Maddy, take Spot to the nurse, if you would." Maddy nodded. Mr. Henry then turned his attention to the top of the slide. "Russell, please come down here. "

"Yes, sir," Russell yipped as he slid down the slide, landing on all fours in the mud with his tail wagging, sending mud flying all over the other students.

"I helped Spot go down the slide. Do I get my star now?" Russell asked as he ran up to Mr. Henry and placed his muddy paws on him as his tailed wagged.

"Shoving a student is NOT helping," Mr. Henry said with his paws on his hips. Russell dropped back on all fours and lowered his ears and tucked his tail between his legs. Mr. Henry continued, "This is the twice I've had to talk with you. I am not giving up on you, but you will have detention." Mr. Henry said as he wiped mud off his teacher's vest.

Chapter Five
Pop Quiz

"GOOD MORNING, CLASS," MR. Henry barked as he stood at the front of the classroom.

"Good morning, Mr. Henry," the class barked in unison.

Mr. Henry held up a stack of papers and cleared his throat. "Does anyone know what a pop quiz is?"

Maddy was the only pup to raise her paw, and Mr. Henry called on her. "It is a surprise test to see if we were paying attention."

"Very good, Maddy."

All the pups let out a groan as Mr. Henry handed out tests.

"You have until lunch to finish; I will be at my desk if you need anything," Mr. Henry said, placing a quiz on Russell's desk.

After scribbling his answers on his test, he looked at Maddy and smiled. He noticed her test upside down and her nose in her book. He turned to look when he heard a sigh of frustration coming from behind him. He noticed Rocky scratching the top of his head as he struggled with his test. Russell's eyes grew wide—he knew how he could help Rocky.

Russell quickly turned and snatched Rocky's test off his desk, circling his answers for him. Rocky tapped Russell on the shoulder as he attempted to get his test back.

"Give me back my test."

"Almost done." Russell said as he circled Rocky's last answer and wrote a note on the top of Rocky's test.

HeLped By RuSseLL

He wanted to ensure Mr. Henry knew he had helped Rocky. Now he would surely get his star, Russell thought. The lunch bell rang as Russell handed back Rocky's test. He grinned ear to ear as stars danced through his mind. Russell walked briskly with Maddy to the lunchroom with his chin up, feeling rather proud.

"I'm gonna get my gold star, I'm gonna get my gold star." Russell yipped as he bounced circles around Maddy as they walked down the hallway towards the cafeteria.

"That's great, but how?" Maddy asked tilting her head as they stopped at the cafeteria doors.

"I helped Rocky with his quiz."

Maddy looked at him warily. "Are you sure that was a good idea?"

"You'll see when I have a gold star when we get back to class."

"Yeah, or detention," Maddy yipped as they entered the cafeteria.

After lunch, Russell sat at his desk and doodled Super Mutt in his notebook. Russell watched intently as Mr. Henry graded their tests one by one. As he rested his chin on his paws, he could not help slowly drifting off, dreaming he was Super Russ.

"Hot off the press! Get your papers here!"

Super Russ watched the pup peddling his newspapers at the entrance of the grocery store while he sat on the roof of the building across the street. Russell watched as a Dalmatian pushed a pink puppy carriage towards the grocery store door.

"Paper, ma'am?" the pup asked her as he held out a rolled paper.

"Dawson, I would love one," the Dalmatian said as she dug through her coin purse.

He handed her the paper and took her coin. "Thanks, ma'am."

"It has been a quiet night," Super Russ thought as he rested his chin on his paw before pulling out his pocket watch. He stood up and stretched, then stepped on the edge of the ledge and leapt into the air, his cape trailing behind him. Within a flash, he landed on his windowsill and stepped inside. As he walked to the kitchen, he hung his cape and mask on a hook on the wall. Super Russ rubbed his belly, feeling it growl as he opened the cabinet and pulled out an empty bowl and a box of Liver Nips.

"HELPPPP."

Super Russ grinned from ear to ear. "Looks like I'm skipping dinner." He grabbed his cape and mask as he ran towards the window. He unlatched it, pushed it open, and leapt out.

A Shih Tzu pushed her glasses up her nose and started up the stairwell, pausing halfway to catch her breath. Panting, she finally pushed the roof door open and ran towards the large spotlight, the door slamming behind her. "How do I turn this on?" she barked, scratching her head as she looked the light up and down.

"There!" she barked as she flipped the red switch at the back, sending a large beam of white light straight into the apartment window across the street.

"My word!" she gasped as she looked in the apartment window at a large bulldog with a towel around his waist. His hands were over his eyes as he stumbled around his living room, mouthing, "My eyes!"

"Whoops!" she barked, then ran to the back of the light, bit the handle and gave it a tug. The beam lifted and shot into the sky, illuminating the night with a bone-shaped light.

"I hope he gets here soon," she yelped as she paced back and forth, chewing on her pen.

THUD!

The Shih Tzu screamed as she jumped in the air, sending her pen flying before it rolled to a stop at Super Russ' feet.

"You okay, miss?" Super Russ barked as he picked it up and handed her pen back with a smile.

"Yes, thank you." she said as she fumbled with her clipboard as she took the pen.

"Why have you signaled me?" Super Russ asked, flipping off the spotlight.

"Our newspaper van is stolen."

"Where from?"

"Our printers across town, please help. We loaded it with all of tomorrow's papers and the mayor will not be happy if his picture is not on the cover this week"

"I'm on it, miss." Super Russ said. He nodded as he gave her a grin.

Super Russ adjusted his cape and leaped into the air and landed on the tallest building with a thud. He climbed up the radio tower and placed his hands on his temples, activating his super vision as he scanned the horizon.

"Where is the printing house?" he barked to himself, a sign in the distance pulsed as it glowed. "Ah, there it is—*Dogwood Chronicles*." Super Russ pushed himself off the radio tower with his back legs, leaping into the air. He jumped from roof top to roof top until he landed at the rear of the *Dogwood Chronicles*. He looked around at the pothole-filled parking lot.

"There have to be clues here somewhere." He said to himself as he looked around.

He placed his paws on his temples, once more activating his super vision. "The door is still open," he barked as he looked at a stack of newspapers sitting on a dolly just inside the ajarred door. Super Russ looked down and saw a collar laid broken on concrete, he reached down and picked it up and looked at it.

"No name," he barked as he looked around the parking lot some more, spotting something else. "Tire marks." He followed them through the alley to where they met at the main road.

SLAM!

SQUEAL!

Super Russ perked his ears up as he activated his super hearing to locate the direction of the squealing tires. "North!" he barked, then squatted with his back legs and leaped into the air with his paws straight out.

Once airborne, Super Russ placed his paws on his temples, activating his super vision and illuminating a vehicle in the distance. "There! A few miles ahead." He saw a rogue van swerving in and out, barely missing oncoming traffic. Super Russ raced to catch up as his cape whipped in the wind behind him.

SCREECH!

The van made a sharp left turn as pedestrians dove out of the way. The van sped through a construction site, sending workers running for their lives as they dove out of the way of the van. Super Russ used his super vision to see where the van was headed. He noticed the van headed to a lift bridge just up ahead.

Super Russ raced ahead as he flew through the clouds. He landed on the bridge, and ran into the bridge's control room. He held his paw above the big red button, waiting for the van to get closer as watched out of the window of the control room.

"There!" Super Russ barked as he smashed the button. The draw bridge engines whirred to life and the control room vibrated as the bridge began to lift and part in the center. The gap grow larger and Super Russ knew it would either force the van to either stop or jump the gap.

SCREECH!

The van's tired squealed to a stop and Super Russ landed in front of it. "Put your hands up and step out of the van," he barked as he stood with his fists on his hips, cape fluttering in the breeze.

Two masked dogs stepped out of the van with their paws in the air as flashing lights headed towards them. They looked over their shoulders as a large blue K-9 unit van pulled up next to them. A group of Shepard stormed out of the van wearing police uniforms.

"Arrest both those canines," the German Shepherd barked as he pointed at the masked fugitives. Several shepherds handcuffed the rogue dogs before removing their masks.

"We have been looking for you two mutts. Good work, Super Russ," the German Shepard barked as he watched the fugitives get loaded into the back of the squad cars in cuffs. Then, he turned to Super Russ, holding out his paw. "I am Detective Bones. I was recently promoted, so you might see more of me."

"Nice to meet you," Super Russ said as he gave the detective's paw a firm shake.

"How did you catch these jewelry thiefs so quickly?"

"The jewelry thiefs ?"

"These mutts just robbed the jewelry store off Fifth."

"I was just tracking down a missing newspaper van."

Super Russ watched Detective Bones write in his spiral notebook. "Looks like they stole the van to rob the jewelry store." Detective Bones put his notepad back in his pocket. Super Russ followed Detective Bones to the van and he opened the van door, sending jewel-encrusted collars and bows pouring onto the bridge. Super Russ leaned into the back of the van to look as he noticed a pup was huddled in the back of the van.

"I know that pup," Super Russ barked. "He was selling newspapers outside the grocery store this morning...his name is Dawson."

Detective Bones reached in and lifted the young pup out of the van, knocking a newspaper onto the ground. Super Russ picked up the newspaper and read the headline. "Mayor Re-elected After Super Russ Collab."

A crowd had gathered on the bridge as the K-9 unit cleaned up all the jewelry. A reporter approached Detective Bones. "Detective, can you tell us how you caught the bandits?"

"Super Russ stopped the fugitives and saved the hostage," Detective Bones barked as he pointed towards Super Russ and started clapping. The crowd joined in.

"Super Russ!"

"Super Russ!"

"Russ!"

"Russell. Russell, please step outside with me," Mr. Henry barked as he held a rolled-up paper. Russell got up and followed Mr. Henry to the front of the room. His tail wagged as he walked by the star chart and looked at the space next to his name. "Rocky, you as well." Mr. Henry barked as he held the door open for both of the pups.

"Rocky gets a gold star, too?" Russell said as he followed Rocky and Mr. Henry out into the hall. Mr. Henry held up Rocky's pop quiz, pointing to where Russell signed his name at the top. "Do either of you want to explain this?"

"I helped. Do I get my gold star now?" Russell asked, grinning ear to ear.

"Absolutely not," Mr. Henry barked, placing his paw on his hip as he handed Rocky his quiz. "Cheating is NOT helping. You made Rocky fail his quiz. I am sending you both to detention. You two can make up your quiz there, and no helping each other."

Russell tucked his tail between his legs and whimpered as he headed down the he hall towards the detention room as Rocky followed beside him, both with their tails tucked between their legs as their heads hung low.

"Thanks, Russell," Rocky barked under his breath as he walked ahead. Russell said nothing as he trailed behind him.

In detention, Russell scribbled the answers down on his quiz, then turned his paper over and doodled Super Mutt as he thought about not getting his gold star. He yawned and slowly his eyes closed.

"Russell!"

Russell looked up at Mr. Henry standing over him with one paw on his hip and the other pointing at his quiz. "Are you finished?"

Russell nodded, and his voice cracked as he spoke. "Yes sir."

"Come with me. Your mom is waiting outside for you."

Chapter Six

Cheater, Cheater

THE NEXT MORNING, RUSSELL adjusted his cape as he looked at his reflection in the bedroom mirror. He let out a sigh and unfastened his cape, allowing it to fall to the floor. "Russ," his mother called, "breakfast is ready."

Russell scooted himself up to the table as he watched his mom place his favorite cereal in front of him. But he pushed his bowl away. "I'm not hungry, Ma."

"Are you feeling sick?" His mom barked as she placed her paw on his forehead to feel if it was warm.

"I'm fine, Ma."

Russell ears perked up as he heard the bus pull up. He scooted out of his chair and headed towards the door. He stared at the hardwood floor as he waited for his mom to open the door.

"Are you forgetting something?"

"No, Ma."

"You're not wearing your cape?"

"I don't want to wear it anymore." Russell sighed as he looked up at her as she opened the door. His mom adjusted his vest as his eyes welled with tears. He wiped his eyes and headed towards the bus.

Russell quietly took his usual seat and watched Maddy as she silently mouthed the words she was reading, flipping the pages of her textbook. Within a few minutes, students were chanting insults at Russell from the back of the bus.

"Cheater, Cheater, cat food eater."

"Run and hide or he will shove you down the slide."

Russell tried his best to ignore the students in the back of the bus, but he found it difficult. Maddy tilted her head and looked Russell up and down.

"You look different."

Russell just sat with his arms crossed, hoping she would give up on her investigation.

"That's it, no cape today."

"I didn't feel like wearing it to detention"

"It's too bad that you have detention. I like your cape."

Russell didn't even think about being a superhero. He just stared out the window and watched the dog houses go by, wishing he was back home and in his bed. Maddy interrupted his thoughts, pointing to a page in her textbook. "Did you know that service dogs have to be calm, alert, social, and able to perform tasks?"

Russell just nodded as the bus pulled into the school parking lot. He watched Maddy as she headed to class. Then, he headed down the hall to the detention room, where Mr. Henry was waiting for him.

"Good Morning, Russell; follow me."

Russell followed Mr. Henry past the trophy case and to an empty classroom at the end of the hall. "Here we are," Mr. Henry barked as he opened the door and flipped on the lights.

"I wish I was Super Mutt, then I would know how to help." Russell said as he looked up at Mr. Henry.

"Russell, you don't need to be a superhero to help."

Mr. Henry followed Russell to his desk and handed him a book. Russell nodded and watched as Mr. Henry shut the door on his way out. Russell read the cover on the book "Helping Others." He turned to the first page and rested his chin on his paw, he stared out the window as he began to day dream.

"Oh look, it's Super Russ," shouted a bystander as he pointed towards the sky. A dark streak shot across the sky overhead as the bystanders gathered around to watch. Super Russ darted in between the skyscrapers, scanning with his super vision for pups in need. He raised his ears to activate his super hearing, listening for sounds of distress, when he heard distant cries.

"Help! Somebody, please help."

Russell spun around and focused his hearing as he pin pointed the pleas for help. He tilted his head as his ears picked up pulses from the cries in the distance. He placed his hands on his temples and activated his super vision as he scanned the street ahead. He spotted a rogue baby carriage rolling down a steep street with its mother chasing behind.

He gasp as he witnessed the mother struggling to keep up.

"Help, my pup!" she cried again.

Super Pup's eyes grew wide. He flew down to the street, weaving in and out of traffic to catch the stray carriage. Looking ahead, he saw a large trash truck pulling out of the intersection, It was headed straight toward the puppy carriage. He located a rope hanging out of a nearby work truck and flew to grab it. He quickly tied a lasso and gave it a whirl through the air, wrapping the loop around the carriage. Russell planted his paws on the road as he gave the rope a firm pull. His paws dug into the hot asphalt, and the carriage skidded to a stop.

"Whew." Super Russ wiped the sweat off his brow as the pup's mother ran to check on her pup.

"My pup, my pup!"

Russell picked up her whimpering pup and handed it to her. "You best get those carriage breaks repaired, ma'am," Super Russ barked, then looked at his pocket watch. His eyes grew wide as his watch began ringing. *That's strange*, he thought, tapping the glass.

RIINNNGGG.

RIIINNGGGGGGGG.

"Russell," Mr. Henry barked as he held the door open. Russell's eyes snapped open, and he looked around. "Did you hear the bell?"

Mr. Henry gestured to Russell to follow him. Russell jumped up and chased Mr. Henry down the hall to where Mr. Henry stood. "You walk past this trophy case every day, but have you ever looked inside?"

Russell just shook his head, then placed his paws on the glass and peered inside. He looked at dozens of trophies along with plaques, pictures, and ribbons. Russell put his nose to the glass and read the plaque for a brown-haired pup. "Gypsy."

"Ah, I see you found your mom."

"My ma?"

"Yes, she was a four-time consecutive winner of the Juvenile Service Dog Division of the Kennel Kup, and a daydreamer like you."

"Really?"

"No pup has won it four times in a row since then."

"Whoa, I didn't know that."

Mr. Henry looked at his watch as he walked past Russell. "I have a meeting after you head towards the bus."

Russell nodded and took off to find Maddy. She was getting on the bus when he finally caught up. He tapped Maddy on the shoulder and boarded the steps behind her. "How was class?" he asked.

"It was okay, not as fun without you."

Maddy sat on the seat next to him. She unzipped her bag and pulled out a few papers, handing them to Russell.

"Notes from the lesson you missed."

"Thank you." Russell said and gave her a smile. A few of the students chanted their usual teases at the back of the bus. One said, "Hey Maddy, don't let Russell shove you off the bus."

Several students laughed and snorted. Russell looked out the window and crossed his arms. He thought about how he shoved Spot off the slide. He could still hear all the pups on the playground laughing at him.

"Hey Russ, guess what..." Maddy pointed at her textbook, waiting for Russell to respond.

"Let me guess, another useless fact."

"Maybe if you focused less on Super Mutt and more on your textbook, you might understand how to help,"

Maddy huffed as she got up and moved to the empty seat next to Ally. Russell sighed and slumped down. He rested his head on the window as doghouses went by, feeling even more defeated. He daydreamed he was Super Russ and Maddy needed rescuing.

As lightning struck the bridge, the passengers on the bus screamed. The front tire had already broken through the wood planking of the bridge as the bus driver attempted to free the bus by stepping on the gas. But the bus refused to move, the tires on the back spinning, sending smoke into the air. The second tire broke through the wood planks, leaving the front of the bus dangling over the rapids below. The bus driver frantically called for help on his radio.

"Mayday—Mayday! School bus with students in trouble at Doglick River bridge. I repeat: mayday, mayday!"

The bus driver unfastened his seatbelt and braced himself to keep from sliding against the windshield. "Students, I need you to climb to the back of the bus. Slowly," the driver added.

The bus driver and the students slowly climbed towards the back of the bus. The bus swayed with every move they made. Maddy stayed ducked down as she held on to her seat. The bus driver pushed open the rear door and the rain came pouring in.

He told the students to exit one at a time as he helped them out of the bus. Once all the students were safely on the wooden bridge, it began raining even harder.

"Is that everyone?" the bus driver asked before counting the pups as they huddled against him.

"Maddy is still on the bus!" Ally said, pointing. The bus driver stuck his head into the bus and looked around for Maddy. He spotted her paws clinging to the back of a seat.

"Maddy," he called, "I need you to climb to the back door. Can you do that?"

"I can't."

"Yes, you can."

Maddy dug her claws in as she climbed over her seat towards the back of the bus, her paws and arms shaking. The wind rocked the bus back and forth and she trembled, struggling to grip the wet bus seats.

"That's good. You'll be with us if you do that four more times."

As Maddy climbed over the next seat, the wooden bridge creaked and the bus drivers eyes grew wide as he heard a snap, and the bus fell further, dangling by the rear tires. The bus's jolt caused Maddy to fall back to the seat behind her, landing on her back. Maddy rolled over and tried to jump to the next seat but she barley made it as her back paws dangled as she struggled to hold on to the wet seat the rain poured in.

"Help, I'm slipping!" she yelped as she attempted to pull her self up but her arms were to weak. The huddled pups yelped as a flash shot across the sky towards the bridge.

"It's Super Russ!" a pup cheered, watching him fly through the rear of the bus door as a gust of wind caused the driver to stumble, holding his hat on his head.

The driver and students watched the bus rock back and forth with Maddy and Super Russ still inside. Super Russ jumped out of the rear of the bus with Maddy in his paws.

"Super Russ, you are my hero," Maddy said as the bus broke free from the bridge and started to fall to the rapids below. Super Russ gasp as the bus snagged his cape, taking him and Maddy with it.

"NO!" The bus driver said as he peered through the hole in the bridge. He watched as the bus, Maddy, and Super Russ crashed into the river below. All the students huddled together and whined for Maddy and Super Russ, shivering as the rain dripped off their fur.

"There, there pups," the bus driver soothed as he wrapped his arms around the students.

"What about Maddy?" Ally cried as she looked past the bus driver towards the hole in the bridge.

"Let's hope Super Russ can swim," the bus driver said, noticing the blue and red lights flashing in the distance. The lights grew brighter as the sirens grew louder.

THUMP.

The bus driver jumped and looked behind him. Super Russ landed on the bridge, holding a waterlogged Maddy in his arms. All the pups ran up to Super Russ, cheering and shouting his name.

"Super Russ!"

"Super Russ!"

"Russ!"

"Russell!"

The bus driver shook Russell awake.

"Ah!" Russell's eyes snapped open, and he panted as he looked around. The students at the back of the bus laughed as Russell yelped.

"This is your stop." The bus driver walked to the front of the bus and opened the door. Russell grabbed his things and fumbled his way to the front. He looked back at Maddy before stepping off the bus.

Russell's mom was waiting for him, holding the door as he sauntered towards the front door. "Want me to cook your favorite dinner?"

"I'm not hungry." Russell said as he walked past her and towards the stairs.

Russell threw his service vest on the floor and crawled into bed. Feeling lonelier than ever, he replayed the day's events. He stared at his bedroom wall, thinking of all the things he'd done wrong. He grabbed his Super Mutt plush and looked at it before throwing it onto the hardwood floor.

"Super Mutt is about to start."

Russell looked at his mom, who stood in his doorway.

"I don't want to watch it," he mumbled as he rolled away and covered his head with his blanket.

His mom noticed his Super Mutt doll laying on the floor and picked it up before sitting on the side of his bed.

"You know, even Super Mutt has bad days," she gently barked as she laid his plush next to him.

"I know, like the time he got trapped in the stinky sewer." Russell sat up and grabbed his plush, wiping a tear off his cheek as he looked at his mom.

"Yes, I remember the sewer episode. Didn't he make a few changes and then he could escape?"

"At least his friend still likes him." Russell covered his nose with his blanket as his mom headed towards his door.

"You and Maddy have a falling out?"

"Yeah, and now she won't sit with me."

"Have you tried apologizing?" his mom said as she picked up his cape and folded it.

"No, Ma." Russell said as he watched her place it on his dresser. She turned his light off and went to check on supper when Russell stopped her.

"Hey, Ma?"

"Yes, honey?"

"Does apologizing work for teachers, too?" Russell said as he looked at his paws as he fiddled with his Super Mutt quilt.

"Yes, honey, even for teachers."

"I don't know if I can."

"If you cannot find the words, you can always write a letter." She said as she pulled his door halfway closed.

A letter, he thought to himself as he covered up with his blanket and thought about what his mom said. He also thought about what

Mr. Henry had told him while at the trophy case. He especially thought about what Maddy had said: "If you paid more attention to your textbook and less on Super Mutt, you might know how to help."

Russell repeated Maddy's words. Finally, his eyes closed. Tomorrow, he knew what he needed to do.

Chapter Seven
Hemmed Capes

RUSSELL JUMPED OUT OF bed just as the sun peeked through his window. He let out a stretch as his paws felt the cool hardwood floor as he looked at his clock. When Russell opened his door, he saw a box sitting in the hallway. He tilted his head and looked at the box. He wiped the dust off the top and read the words written in faded black marker: Gypsy's School Tapes. His eyes grew wide as he thought about the moment he had with Mr. Henry at the trophy case. Russell lifted the lid of the box, revealing a dozen or so tapes inside. He let out a sneeze as he dug through the dusty contents before picking out the tape labeled Service Canine Training Video 1.

"Whoa." Russell said as he wiped the dust off the tape before running downstairs and straight to the living room TV. He turned the TV on and slid the tape into the player. As he waited for the tape to play, he ran to the kitchen and grabbed a bowl and box of Liver Nips. He poured himself a bowl and sat directly in front of the television.

"You're up early on a Saturday." Russell's mom yawned as she came downstairs and looked at the clock on the wall.

"I have a lot to study." Russell's tail wagged as he took a bite of his LiverNips as he sat directly in front of the TV with his nose a few inches from the screen.

"You shouldn't sit so close to the TV." His mom said as he walked past him towards the kitchen.

"I don't want to miss anything." Russell said as he scooted closer to the television as she poured herself a hot cup of spring water.

Russell stared at the television, trying not to blink as he watched tape after tape until his mom made him take a break.

"Lunch is ready." She said as she sat a box of Beef N' Cheese Nips on the kitchen table as she held two bowls.

"I'm not hungry, I have to much studying to do."

"You need to eat lunch, those tapes aren't going anywhere." She said as she pulled his chair out to encourage him to climb up.

"I got to grab something first, Ma."

Russell sprinted upstairs and came trotting back down with his cape in his mouth. He dropped it at her paws and asked, "Can you trim my cape, so I won't trip on it anymore?"

"After lunch, I'll work on it." She said as she picked it up and placed on the table. Russell sat down and had lunch with his mom as he talked about what he learned on the first video.

Russell's mom worked on hemming his cape as Russell watched tape after tape. His mom looked at the clock when she noticed the sun was setting through the kitchen window.

"Your show is about to start."

"Not tonight, Ma. I have more tapes to watch."

Russell watched tapes until he fell asleep on the carpet. His mom picked him up and carried him to bed. Russell couldn't help but dream he was Super Russ.

Super Russ stood at the starting line, his heart racing in anticipation of the buzzer.

BUZZZZ!

Super Russ took off across the artificial turf to his first obstacle. He wove in and out of the poles with ease, then grabbed the rope ladder and climbed up to the top of the brick wall. He threw his leg over and climbed down the other side. The crowd cheered.

Once over the wall, he sprinted to the next obstacle, where he dropped on his belly and crawled through the tunnel in record time. He jumped to his paws as he exited the tunnel. The crowd roared to life as he sprinted to the mock crosswalk. He slammed his paw on the walk button and escorted the pup across the mock street.

He made it through the next few obstacles in record time. Then, he turned the corner to the last obstacle. Super Russ dove into the in-ground pool and swam to the pup struggling in the middle.

Super Russ grabbed the young pup and looked around for anything that might help. He spotted a floating life preserver, he put the pup inside, and pulled him to the edge of the pool. The crowd cheered once more.

Super Russ stood with the other contestants when a Poodle in a suit came to the stage. The Poodle cleared his throat. "Gentledames and gentlemutts, today marks our seventy-fifth Kennel Kup awards. This event is sponsored by Liver Nips, our loyal sponsor for the last two decades."

The speaker paused for the cheers to subside. When the crowd settled down, he said, "Our third place trophy goes to...Benny Barkley."

Benny Barkley walked to the Poodle and took his trophy as he said his thanks. The crowd cheered as the Poodle clapped for Benny.

"Thank you. Our second place trophy goes to...Lola Longtail."

The crowd cheered as the white dog accepted her trophy. The Poodle cleared his throat.

"We have saved the best for last: our first place trophy goes to...Super Russ, who completed each obstacle in record time."

The crowd drowned out the Poodle as they chanted.

"Super Russ!"

"Super Russ!"

"Russ!"

Russell stretched and yawned as the sun gleamed through the window. Then he looked at his clock.

"I must have been tired, its noon already."

Russell walked to his door and noticed his red cape hanging on the nob. It was newly hemmed. He put it on and walked to the mirror to admire it. He noticed it no longer dragged on the ground. After he finished with the mirror, he grabbed a pen and paper out of his backpack. He had some apology letters to write.

Chapter Eight
Helping Paw

As Russell waited for the bus to pull up, he held the letter he'd written for Maddy. Russell looked back at his mom and she gave him a smile and a nod to encourage him. The students in the back started taunting Russell as he boarded the bus.

"Cheater, cheater, cat food eater."

"Run and hide before he shoves you down the slide."

Ignoring the students with his chin up, Russell walked to where Maddy was sitting and held out the letter.

"Watch out, Maddy, he might shove you off the bus." a student taunted but Russell ignored him.

She took the letter and Russell sat by himself, hoping she would accept his apology. He occasionally would glance back to see if she had opened it or read it.

Later at school, Russell stood at the star chart, looking at all the stars next to everyone's name. He put his paw on the empty spot next to his.

Maddy elbowed him. "Hey, you have until Friday. No sweat." She said as she smiled.

"You are not angry with me?"

"I know you were having a hard time," she said.

Russell and Maddy took their seats. His tail wagged at the sight of Maddy sitting next to him. He looked over at her and admired the pink bow in her golden fur.

Mr. Henry walk to the front of the classroom and wrote on the board: Research Day.

"Today, class, we will spend the day in the library studying the history of service dogs." Mr. Henry gestured for the class to follow him. Everyone yipped and wagged their tails. Russell kept thinking to himself that Friday wasn't so far off. Mr. Henry walked past.

Service Dogs in the Community. Russell flipped to the first page and read. The more he read, the more his eyes closed until he drifted off.

"Whoa, look!" a bystander shouted as a black and red blur shot past him, knocking the bystander off his feet and onto the sidewalk.

Super Russ was using his super vision to locate pups in need when he heard a large metal screeching, followed by screams. He darted through the city, in and out of buildings, towards the source of the commotion. He shot up to the top of the tallest building and put his paws on his temple, activating his super vision. In the distance, he noticed smoke billowing up from a train that was speeding down the tracks. In a flash, Super Russ was at the window of the train and peered in at the conductor, who was frantically pulling knobs and pushing buttons as sweat poured down his forehead.

"IT'S NO USE!" the conductor shouted to Super Russ out the small window. Super Russ looked around for anything that might help stop the train when he spotted a sharp curve up ahead.

"This is not good."

Super Russ shot ahead of the train and planted his feet on the tracks. He held his out his paws, closed his eyes, and braced for the train to hit him. When the train struck him, the force was so strong it pushed him along the track as pieces of the track broke off, flying into the air. He dug his paws deeper into the track until the train came to a stop just before the sharp curve. All the passengers chanted as Super Russ opened his eyes and looked at all the passengers cheering out the train windows.

"Super Russ!"

"Super Russ!"

"Russ!"

"Russell," Mr. Henry barked. Russell's eyes shot open and looked frantically around at all his classmates laughing.

"Who is Super Russ?" one of classmate laughed as the others giggled. Russell's cheeks turned red, and he slumped down in his chair.

Maddy looked up from her book. "Ignore them." She smiled at Russell, then turned her page, pointing as she said, "Hey Russ, did you know...never mind."

"No, tell me, I wanna know."

"Therapy dogs bring happiness and comfort to schools, nursing homes, and hospitals."

"You must be my therapy dog."

Maddy's cheeks turned red as she fought back a smile. Russell went back to reading his book until the last bell rang.

Russell placed his notebook in his backpack as Maddy stood next to the table, waiting for him. All the other students headed towards the library doors.

"Wait!" Ally gasp as she dug around the desk, panting as she looked under books and papers. "Where is it?"

Russell walked over. "Whatcha looking for?" He watched Ally fumble with her books and papers. She gasped as she dug through her backpack.

"My inhaler, I just had it."

"I will help you."

Russell crawled under the table, looking under the chairs for Ally's inhaler. He then searched the tops of the chairs, one by one, to make sure he didn't overlook it when he spotted something red out the corner of his eye. He spotted the inhaler sitting just behind the table next to the bookshelf when he reached and grabbed and held it up.

"You found it!"

Russell crawled out from under the table with her inhaler in his mouth and smiled. He handed Ally her inhaler, and she quickly took a puff.

"Thank you...for helping me,"

A huge grin spread across Russell's face. He elbowed Maddy and mouthed the word "help." Maddy's tail wagged as she gave him a smile. As Ally returned her belongings to her backpack, they overheard the librarian on the phone.

"Mr. Henry, you still have students in the library."

Maddy threw her backpack on her shoulders and turned towards Ally and Russell. "I bet we missed the bus."

They headed towards the exit as the doors flew open. Mr. Henry marched in. "You three, please tell me you have a good reason for missing your bus."

"I lost my inhaler, and they were helping me find it."

"Looks like I will have to give you three a ride home." Mr. Henry said as he stood with his paws on his hips.

Russell, Maddy, and Ally followed Mr. Henry out into the main hall. As they made their way to the parking lot, they passed a large display case next to the principal's office.

Russell stopped and looked at his mom's trophies in the case again, thinking of what Mr. Henry had told him. Maddy looked into the case to see what he was seeing. "Whatcha looking at?"

"My ma."

"Gypsy is your ma?"

"Yep."

"Can I meet her?"

"Yeah."

Chapter Nine
Missing Star

"Slow down, Russ," Maddy barked as she struggled to keep up with Russell, who was rushing down the hall.

"I got to see my star." Russell raced through the crowded hallway, weaving through the students. As she opened the classroom door open, Russell ran past her to the star chart. He looked down the list of names until he found his.

"What?" Russell barked.

"Oh," Maddy sighed as she noticed a blank space next to Russell's name. Maddy noticed the look of disappointment on Russell's face.

"Hey, I wouldn't worry. I bet Mr. Henry just hadn't put it on yet."

"Yeah, you're probably right."

Russell kept looking over his shoulder at the other students. "I wish I could find more students to help," Russell mumbled as he sat back down at his desk. Maddy looked up from her book and pushed her glasses up. "Did you know service dogs can have unique abilities?" she gently barked.

"That's cool. I wish I had super hearing like Super Mutt; then I could be the best at the assignment." Russell raised one ear up to her, exaggerating listening.

"That would be cool. I wish I could fly." Maddy said as she placed her book on her lap and put her paws straight out, swaying back and forth as they both chuckled.

"Do not worry, we have until Friday to get our stars," Maddy replied, pushing her glasses back up her nose. Russell sat quietly as he watched the bird on the windowsill. He started imagining he was Super Russ again.

BOOM!

CREAK!

SMASH!

An explosion shook the Dogwood Mall with such force the sign toppled over, landing on a parked car, flattening it. Bystanders ran around, confused, screaming at the chaos.

A dark flash appeared in the distance, unafraid, and headed towards the source of the explosion. "It is Super Russ!" one bystander shouted, pointing towards the sky.

Super Russ hovered above the mall, scanning with his super vision to locate the source of the explosion. He scanned the food court, then each restaurant one by one until he found the source: a leaking gas line still rattling and ablaze. Super Russ searched the parking lot for the valve to turn it off when another explosion shook the mall. The roof over the food court and exits collapsed, trapping fleeing shoppers inside. Super Russ' ears perked up at the sound of the shoppers' cries. He flew around the mall, once more frantically searching for the valve before focusing his super vison on the basement of the mall.

"There it is," he shouted. He flew through the crack in the mall's wall before stopping at the emergency stairwell. Super Russ slid his paws between the doors of the elevator, growling as he forced them apart. "Let's see where this takes us." After jumping into the elevator shaft, he let himself fall and land at the bottom. Super Russ stood with his feet planted and place both his paws on his temple to help focus his super vision. He scanned left and right as he located the shut-off valve. He turned the valve, but the pipe rattled even harder.

BOOM.

CRASH!

Super Russ smashed into a shelf across the basement, sending paint cans rolling across the floor as a wooden shelf broke free, landing on his head. He used a stack of boxes to help hold himself until the ringing in his ears subsided and was replaced by the sound of the shoppers' cries.

Super Russ looked at the shredded gas valve as he rubbed the knot on his head. He ran back to the elevator and flew back up to the top floor. Super Russ scanned the area. He counted the number of shoppers. One. Two...seven. He saw one shopper trapped beneath a bookcase while the rest were standing beside a fountain that had cracked in the explosion. Super Russ ran to the pinned shopper.

"Please, help. My paw is stuck," the shopper cried as Super Russ lifted the shelf over his head and threw it across the bookstore. Super Russ grabbed the shopper and flew him up through the hole in the ceiling above the fountain. The remaining trapped shoppers stood huddled by the fountain as they watched Super Russ fly up and out of the hole in the ceiling. They watched and began to cheer as Super Russ flew back into the hole and grabbed them one by one. Once the last canine was safety in the parking lot, the crowd of bystanders began to shout.

"Super Russ!"

"Super Russ!"

"Russ!"

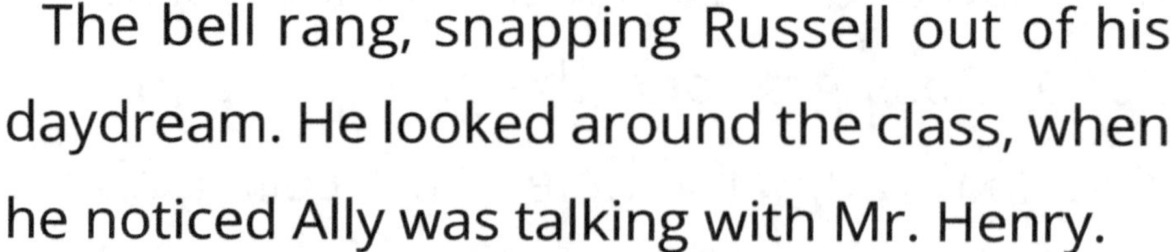

The bell rang, snapping Russell out of his daydream. He looked around the class, when he noticed Ally was talking with Mr. Henry.

"This is it," Russell whispered to Maddy. Maddy nodded at Russell and watched as Mr. Henry walk to the front of the room towards the star chart. stop and then turn and pulled the projector screen.

"Today, class, we are going to watch a video about types of service dogs in the community and how they help."

Maddy took out a notebook and pencil as the movie started. She just shrugged as Russell looked at her. Russell placed his chin on his paw and looked at the star chart and sighed.

The movie ended as the bell rang, and Russell followed Maddy outside. He sighed. "I'm happy I helped Ally, but I was hoping to get my star."

"I'm sorry, Russ," Maddy said as she scooted towards the bus window. "I bet you will have one tomorrow."

"What if I don't and I fail?"

"Ally won't let that happen. I bet she will say something."

"I hope so."

During dinner with his mom, Russell pushed his kibble around his bowl, as he thought about not getting his star for helping Ally.

"What's bothering you?" his mom said as she looked at him pushing his kibble around.

"I helped Ally when she lost her inhaler." Russell said as he placed his paw in his chin.

"That's great, honey."

"Yeah, but I didn't earn the gold star." Russell said as he pushed his kibble around with his spoon.

"I didn't earn my gold star the first week, either." his mom said as she smiled at him.

"You didn't?" Russell tilted his head to the side as he looked at his mom.

"Nope, I didn't. After some practice, I caught up enough to even compete in the Kennel Kup." she nodded and took a bite of her kibble.

Russell ate his dinner as he read the back of the cereal box over and over. "No one found her," he said as he pointed to the back of his Liver Nips.

"I know, her parents were friends of your father's. They called this morning and are worried sick."

"Why did they call?"

"Because your father was a search and rescue dog. They asked if I knew anyone who could help find their newborn pup after she wondered off from a birthday party at the Pawter's house."

"Dad was a search and rescue dog?"

"He sure was, he would help find missing and injured pups and dogs."

"What happened to him?"

Russell stared as his mom as she placed her fork down and looked at him. She sighed.

"During a snowstorm, he was helping rescue some dogs and their pups who were trapped in an avalanche at the now abandoned ski resort. He never made it home."

Russell noticed a tear fall from his mother's cheek and scooted down out of his chair and climbed into her lap, giving her a lick on the cheek. "Your father would be so proud of you, gold star or not," she said as she nuzzled him. Russell's eyes welled up as he buried his face in his mom's fur.

Chapter Ten
Skipping School

T‍HE NEXT DAY AT school, Russell stepped off the bus and stopped in his tracks. He held his nose in the air and sniffed. "You smell that?"

Maddy followed, the door closing behind her. She sniffed the air. "No, what is it?"

"It's a smell I've never smelled before."

Russell took off running towards the gate, and Maddy ran to catch up. She watched Russell sniff the asphalt and then the air, continuously moving towards the gate.

"Where are you going?"

"To check it out."

Russell pushed the gate open, looked both ways, and headed across the street. Maddy grabbed Russell's cape with her teeth and planted her feet on the asphalt. Russell ignored her pleas to head back as he dragged Maddy across the street.

"We better get back to class."

"It is coming from that alley. Let go!" Russell placed his back foot on Maddy's face, pushing her off of his cape.

"Hey!" Maddy yelped, rubbing her nose. Russell sniffed around the alley, still searching for the smell. Russell barked as he made it to the end of the alley.

"It's coming from that field."

"We should not go into Mr. Pawter's farm." Maddy pleaded.

But Russell just laid down and crawled under the barbed wire fence and into the cornfield. "Come on, we're getting close. I can smell it!"

Russell waved at Maddy to follow before he took off through the cornfield with his nose to the ground. Maddy climbed under the fence to catch up.

"You can't smell that? The smell is getting stronger," he said.

"All I smell is corn, and the Liver Nips you ate this morning. Can we PLEASE go back now?"

"Not yet," Russell barked as he headed towards the tractor that sat in the field. He wanted to climb it to see above the corn.

"Give me a boost."

Maddy gave Russell a boost, and he climbed onto the tractor seat, looking around and sniffing the air.

"Whoa."

"What do you see?"

"Everything, wait..."

Sniff.

Sniff, Sniff.

"The smell is coming from the barn," Russell barked as he started climbing down from the tractor, but he lost his footing when he stepped on his cape and fell.

"OOF!" Maddy gasped as Russell landed on top of her. Russell got up, then put his paws out and helped Maddy up.

"I've never skipped school before," she said, dusting the dirt off her fur and following Russell towards the barn.

"We just started school."

They both laughed as they made it to the front of the barn. Russell put his nose up and sniffed. "Can you smell it now?"

He opened the barn door and looked inside. Maddy covered her nose as she entered behind him. "If you mean manure, I smell it."

Russell put his nose to the barn floor as he frantically sniffed around to find the source of the smell. "AAHHH CHOOO!" Russell sneezed as he sniffed the pile of hay, causing Maddy to jump and scream.

"You scared me!" Maddy placed her paw on her chest, feeling her heart race while Russell sniffed around until his nose led him to a set of wooden stairs.

"Up here."

Russell climbed the stairs, and Maddy quickly followed. They both sniffed around as they made it to the barn loft.

"AH!" Maddy yelped as she walked through a cobweb that hung just over the stairs. Russell laughed as his is nose then led him to an enormous pile of loose hay.

"It's in the hay!"

Maddy and Russell dug through the hay as they searched for the source of the smell.

"Something moved in there !" Maddy pointed to where she was digging. Russell took over digging in her spot when he felt something. As he pulled back the hay, they both looked at a newborn terrier pup shivering as she huddled in the hay, sucking on her thumb.

"Hi there," Maddy whispered to the little pup.

"We are here to help," Russell whispered as he held out his paw for the pup to take. The pup took Russell's paw and climbed out of the hay.

"What's your name?" Maddy asked the pup, but the pup just sat there sucking her thumb, shivering from the cold loft.

"Mama." Trixie said as she reached out for Russell. Russell took her hand as his eyebrows raised, suddenly remembering, "Her name is Trixie...she's the missing pup from the back of the LiverNips box."

"How long has she been missing?" Maddy said as she followed Russell towards the stairs.

"My mom told me she has been missing since the party at the Pawter's house."

He held the pup's hand as they made it down the stairs and back to the barn doors. Maddy slid the doors closed behind them and followed Russell and the pup back through the cornfield.

Maddy said, "Let's get back. Mr. Henry will know what to do."

"Sounds good," Russell agreed. He held the young pup's paw, guiding her through the cornfield a step at a time. Maddy stuck close to them as they weaved in and out of the stalks of corn. Russell used his nose to retrace his steps, but Maddy was unsure which way was back.

They stepped out of the cornfield and into the edge of the alley. Russell squeezed under the barbed wire and Maddy picked up the pup. She carefully handed her off to Russell through the fence, so the pup wouldn't get poked by the barbed wire.

"I will run ahead and get Mr. Henry," Maddy barked.

"Too late, there he is."

Russell pointed towards the bus driver talking with Mr. Henry. Russell and Maddy headed down the alley towards the street. The pup started lagging as her legs grew tired, but Russell kept a hold of her paw, guiding her the whole way.

Russell and Maddy watched as Mr. Henry spotted them. The pup huddled up to Russell as he made it across the street to the sidewalk where Mr. Henry stood.

"We are so dead," Maddy whispered to Russell.

"The bus driver called me. What are you two doing out here?"

Mr. Henry tapped his paw as he watched Maddy attempt to answer before Russell interrupted. "It's not her fault. She tried to make me come back, but I didn't listen."

"Why are you out here?" Mr. Henry asked again.

Russell swallowed hard as he tried to find the words, but he just pointed to the small pup still gripping his paw as she whimpered.

Mr. Henry gasped. "Oh my, where did you find her?"

"Russell smelled her in the loft of Mr. Pawters barn," Maddy barked.

"She must had took shelter there after the storm, my mom told me she wondered off from a birthday party." Russell added.

"I see and you smelled her all the way from the school?" Mr. Henry said.

Russell just nodded as Mr. Henry stared at the little pup. He picked up the pup, and the pup reached back towards Russell as she whimpered.

"Don't worry Trixie, Mr. Henry will take care of you." Russell said as he patted her head.

Mr. Henry looked surprised. He asked again, "And you smelled her all the way from the school?"

"Yes, sir!"

Russell wagged his tail and adjusted his cape feeling proud.

"I am impressed. You have a nose like a search and rescue dog." Mr. Henry said as he patted the newborn pup on the back, soothing her.

Russell's huge smile spread across his face as he watched Mr. Henry soothing the pup.

"My father was a search and rescue dog."

Mr. Henry nodded. "He would be proud. Now, let's get this girl some help and you two back to class."

From his desk, Russell watched Mr. Henry talking with the principal when he thought about the star chart. He noticed everyone had a star next to their name, except him. Russell just took out his notebook and drew Super Mutt, wearing his red cape. As he drew, he drifted off.

Super Russ' limo pulled up to the paparazzi-filled red carpet. As he watched the crowd, his driver opened his door and the flashes and cheers flooded the limo. Super Russ stepped out of the limo, and the crowd chanted his name.

"Super Russ!"

"Super Russ!"

"Super Russ!"

Super Russ adjusted his cape and waved to the crowd, pausing a few times to pose for the camera before following the red carpet. Super Russ smiled at the large, illuminated stage in the front as he entered the theater. He found his seat marked with a reservation sign and looked around at the crowded theatre at all the prominent figures. Super Russ took his seat as the music played and the curtains opened. He watched as a beautiful white-haired dog in a long red sequin dress took the stage. She adjusted her microphone, cleared her throat, and spoke.

"Check, one, two. Check, one, two, three. Welcome everyone to the ninety-fifth Service Dog Awards."

Super Russ clapped along with the cheering crowd. He watched as the red-haired dog handed out an award to a group of firefighting Dalmatians who'd recently saved a blazing orphanage.

"Good job," Super Russ mumbled to himself, clapping along with the cheering audience.

"We saved the best for last," the red-haired beauty said as she opened her golden starred envelope. "The Service Dog of the Year Award goes to..."

Super Russ didn't take his eyes off her as she fumbled with the envelope.

"The winner is...Super Russ!"

She shouted into the microphone as the crowd roared. Super Russ started up the stairs to the stage. He reached for the award but couldn't grab it just as the crowd started chanting again.

"Super Russ!"
"Super Russ!"
"Russ!"

"Russell."

Mr. Henry's voice snapped Russell out of his daydream. Russell's eyes widened as he looked around. "Yes, sir?"

"I see Super Russ made a reappearance," a classmate teased as others laughed. Russell looked at Mr. Henry standing at the star chart and his heart raced as his eyes widened.

Mr. Henry reached into his folder and grabbed out a star and placed it next to Maddy's name. As he watched him put a star next to his name, Russell tilted his head and wagged his tail and he couldn't sit still. Mr. Henry put another star next to his name, and Russell's heart pounded as Mr. Henry walk to the front of the room.

"Congratulations, class. Every one of you earned their stars for helping other students. However, Russell and Maddy also earned an extra one for helping a lost pup in the community." Mr. Henry began clapping and all the students joined in. Maddy grinned at Russell as he stared at the star chart.

"Looks like Super Russ got two stars."

"And so did his sidekick."

The End

Chapter Eleven

Max Maxwell Episode 17: Part 2

"MR. MAXWELL, YOU HAVE an unmarked envelope in your mail," his assistant said in her usual squeaky voice as she shut his office door behind her. Mr. Maxwell grabbed the envelope and poured the contents on the desk. He jumped out of his chair when he saw a diamond-studded collar with a gold name tag that read *Fifi*. His heart raced as he opened the letter, unsure if his companion was still alive.

The composed the letter of magazine cutouts read:

If YOu wAnT TO C HEr aGaIN

BRiNg 2 MILlIoN tO SuBWay STaTiOn oN 10tH

aT mIDnIGhT. cOmE AlOnE oR ElSe.

Max Maxwell's heart raced as he snarled, attempting to hold back a howl. He flipped the letter over and noticed it was written on the back of an electric bill. Max read the name and address at the top. He stood up and walked to his filing cabinet and began to dig through his files.

"I know it is here somewhere." Max Maxwell barked as he tossed the files on the floor.

"Mr. Maxwell, your two o'clock meeting has arrived." Sassy said as he stood watching him.

Max Maxwell held up a red file. "Here it is!" he barked as he showed the red file to her and opened it. Max Maxwell nodded as he walked to his desk with his nose in the file. He closed the file and laid it on his desk. He stuffed the letter and collar back into the envelope and grabbed the employee file and handed it to Sassy.

"Cancel my meeting" he said as he put on his black trench coat and grabbed his keys hanging by his office door.

"Also call the detectives and give them that envelope and file."

"Where are you going, Mr. Maxwell?" She asked as he opened the door. He paused and turned towards her.

"To find Fifi."

"What do I tell the detectives, Mr. Maxwell?" She said as she shuffled behind him in her tall heels.

Max Maxwell stopped at the elevator, pushed the button and turned to Sassy.

"Everything you know." He said as he stepped inside the elevator.

Once the elevator door closed, he reached into his pocket and put on his mask, then took off his coat and unbuttoned his shirt, revealing a red M on his suit. He neatly folded his clothes and stashed them in the hidden compartment in the elevator. Super Mutt adjusted his cape as the elevator doors opened at the roof. He walked the fire escape and climbed down and he sprinted to his car.

Once down the highway, he pushed a button on his steering wheel and his car shifted from a tan sedan to a black sports car with black tinted windows.

Within a few minutes, Super Mutt pulled into his past employee's apartment. In a flash, he stood at the apartment door. Before Super Mutt could knock, the door opened and the sound of yipping pups filled the hallway. A young pup carrying trash stepped out. His eyes grew wide at the sight of Super Mutt, and he dropped his trash bag on the floor.

"Is your father home?" Super Mutt asked as he tried to peer through the door of the apartment.

"Nah, I mean, no, Super Mutt, sir." The young pup said as he stared at the M on Super Mutts suit.

"Do you know where he is?" The young pup nodded and turned and pointed back at his apartment.

"No, but my mom is here."

A woman holding a newborn pup came to the door, another pup clinging to her leg. "Can I help you?"

Super Mutt said, "Yes ma'am, I'm looking for Baxter."

"He's out of town for work, won't be back until next month, I'm afraid. What's this about?" she added as she switched her pup to her other arm.

"I'm investigating missing persons. His old employer told me I can find him here." Super Mutt said as he reached into his coat pocket and handed her a picture of Fifi.

"Are you talking about Maxwell Industries?" She asked as she took the picture and gave it a glance.

"Yes ma'am." he said as he put the picture back in his pocket.

"Do you recognizer her?"

"No, and they already accused him of stealing, now of kidnapping?" she huffed as she shook her head.

"Thank you for your time." Super Mutt said. He ran towards the railing and leaped over the stairs. The young pup ran after him and leaned over the railing and shouted down as Super Mutt free fell to the bottom.

"By Super Mutt Sir."

Super Mutt landed on his feet, adjusted his cape and he darted back to his car before peeling out of the parking lot. As he sped towards the subway, Super Mutt put his car on autopilot and dialed his assistant.

"Yes, Mr. Maxwell?"

"Clear my schedule for the rest of the evening."

"Yes, Mr. Maxwell. The detectives just arrived."

"Thanks, Sassy."

Super Mutt hung up as he disengaged the autopilot before pulling behind an old factory and into the alley, where he waited until dark. His ringing phone jolted him awake, and he quickly answered.

"Max Maxwell," a deep voice barked.

"Who is this?" Super Mutt asked.

"The one who has something you're after. There has been a change of plans."

"No, I want her back now."

"Except, Maxwell, you aren't the ones calling shots anymore, now are you?"

Super Mutt gritted his teeth. "When and where?"

"Meet me at the abandoned dog food factory on Old Dogwood drive...and Mr. Maxwell? I suggest you come alone. You wouldn't want me to put Fifi down now, would you?"

Super Mutt hung up and threw his car in reverse, and headed across town. It was late, so it didn't take long. It helped that the police never attempted to stop him as he sped past them.

Super Mutt entered the abandoned factory using the rear entrance and placed his hands on his temple, activating his super vision, he spotted a figure in the office just ahead. He dashed to the door and ripped it from its hinges. The masked figure let out a high-pitched scream as Super Mutt tackled and pinned him to the floor with his back paw on his neck.

"Let's see who you are," Super Russ growled as the masked figured struggled to get free. Super Mutt ripped his mask off, revealing a terrified mutt underneath.

"Baxter." Super Mutt said as he shook his head.

"He—he made me d-do it," Baxter said as he tried to push Super Mutt's foot off his neck.

"Who?"

"The...the...the Poodle."

"I need a name!" Super Mutt growled as he pressed down harder on the mutt's neck.

"It was...Goodfellow."

TO BE CONTINUED

Chapter Twelve

15 Facts About Service Dogs

1. SERVICE DOGS ARE not pets, they are tools for disabled persons.

2. Service dogs are trained to do tasks or work for those with disabilities.

3. Service dogs help the independence of an individual with a disability.

4. Hearing dogs help people who are deaf or hard of hearing.

5. Traditional service dogs help people in wheelchairs, walkers, canes, or crutches by picking up items, turning off lights, and holding items.

6. Seizure dogs help by alerting their handler to oncoming seizures.

7. Balance/walk dogs help their partners with walking and balancing.

8. Social dogs can help disabled children learn skills before they are old enough for a service dog of their own.

9. Therapy dogs work with therapists, educators, and volunteers who visit nursing homes and hospitals.

10. Do not interact with a service dog.

11. Do not ask to pet a service dog.

12. Do not ask personal medical information.

13. Respect the service dog's personal space.

14. If you are afraid of dogs, remain calm. Do not yell or scream.

15. A business cannot deny a service dog from entering.

Acknowledgements

I want to acknowledge my dad, who believed I could do this, and to Russell, my late dog; without him this book would not exist.

Also By

Kevin Went to Heaven-2022

The Tatertot Napping Potato-2023

Ms. Riley's Costume Trunk- 2023

Mabel the Thanksgiving Turkey- 2023

The Land of The Flying Whales-2022

Bushcraft Coloring Book-2023

About the Author

K.A.Marabel is an American writer who spends most of her time working as a caregiver to the elderly and disabled. When she is not caring for others, she spends her time writing children's chapter books and picture books. *The Adventures of Russell the Service Dog* is her first children's chapter book.

K.A.Marabel

P.O.Box 128

Brodhead Kentucky, 40409

Books.marabel@gmail.com